Meet The All Stars

Nick's Very First Day of Baseball

Dedication:

To make a dream come true, you need a lot of help, and I have been lucky enough to receive more than my fair share. This help began at home when I was a kid, where I learned the ropes of the family business along with innumerable life lessons. Now, years later, I continue to receive inspiration at home as a husband and father, and from the community that supports our family business. The town of Woodstock, New York has always been incredibly generous to me, and it has proved to be the perfect place to hatch and nurture my ideas for this book and bring them to fruition. It is full of remarkably talented people, the reach of whose kindness has spread as far as California and Canada, and many places in between. I dedicate this first book to them and to everyone who made it possible, especially the kids who were there on my very first day as a new coach—the day which sent me on this incredible journey.

CLARENS PUBLISHING

1. Children's 2. Sports 3. Baseball 4.Non-Fiction 5. Educational 6. Historical 7. Kids 8. Tball

ISBN: 978-0-9863493-0-0

Library of Congress Control Number:

2015931423

Did you know that the Library of Congress number is like your very own cell phone number? No one else can have the same number. Every library in the entire United States can find this book by asking for this number. Libraries are very cool places to visit!!

Printed in the United States of America

Nick's
Very First Day
of Baseball

By Kevin Christofora
Illustrated by Dale Tangeman
www.thehometownallstars.com

Everywhere I went, I dreamed of baseball.

I had baseball all over my brain.

I practiced every afternoon while my parents were busy around the house.

5

I threw crackers to my dog, Yogi.
He's a good catcher.

6

Thursday night, Mom tucked me in at bedtime.
Boy, I can't wait until tomorrow!

Finally, it was Friday, and I arrived at the baseball field. All of my friends were there.

We lined up for our new uniforms.
Coach gave us each a hat, and
the assistant coach gave us a shirt.

Coach blew his whistle for practice to begin, and we all ran over to him. He pulled the hat off my head and said, "Before we start, we need to get all of our names in our hats and on our gloves." Coach wrote NICK inside my hat. Then, he wrote everyone else's names inside of their hats. I really felt like part of the team now.

"Do any of you know the number on the back of your uniform?" Coach asked while he was writing our names. Everyone started making up numbers. Then, we all laughed.

"You are all very silly," Coach said, also laughing while we all tried to see the numbers on our backs.

14

Coach welcomed us to our first real practice. Coach said, "Every practice will start right here, and I will tell you a little about what is going to happen. Every practice we will do warm-ups together as a team, and today I will teach you how to do them. Next practice we will get into some real baseball." Coach told us we all looked great in our new uniforms and he was going to teach us all about baseball and how to have fun.

We got ready for warm ups by dropping our gloves and spreading out. "What's the white hat for?" I asked Coach. "The leader always wears a white hat!" he replied. "Now, let's start with jumping jacks. I am going to show you how to do them."

The coach showed us a fun way to remember how to do jumping jacks. First, we jumped up and put our hands over our head and yelled, "ROCKET." We actually looked like one! Then we jumped back to our starting position with our hands down to our sides and yelled, "PENCIL." "Good job!" Coach said. "Let's do ten of them together as a team."

ROCKET   PENCIL

Now we get to twist like a helicopter. We had to keep our feet still and turn in a circle with our arms out. "Be careful! Not too fast, or you will fly away!" Silly Kareem!

"Last one! Stretches!" We had to stand up straight...up on our tippy-toes and try to reach for the sky. Then, we had to touch our toes. We could not bend our knees. We had to keep our legs straight and count to five real slow. One, two, three, four, five, back up and reach for the clouds. Again, higher! And then down. One, two, three, four, five! We did this five times!

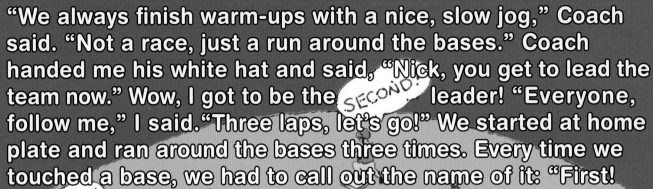

"We always finish warm-ups with a nice, slow jog," Coach said. "Not a race, just a run around the bases." Coach handed me his white hat and said, "Nick, you get to lead the team now." Wow, I got to be the *SECOND* leader! "Everyone, follow me," I said. "Three laps, let's go!" We started at home plate and ran around the bases three times. Every time we touched a base, we had to call out the name of it: "First! *THIRD!* Second! Third! Home!"

While the kids are running, Coach Kevin meets with his assistant coaches to review what they have planned next in practice.

"Okay, kids, today we got our uniforms and had a short practice. At the end of every practice we will meet right here to review what we did. I had a great time. What was your favorite part?"

Shout It Out!

1. What is the name of the game?.................................

2. Why do we play it?...

3. What do we use a glove for?...................................

4. Who does Nick see when he goes to practice?........

5. Which two moves make a jumping jack?...............

6. During warm ups, which base do you
   touch first?..

7. Which base do you touch second?......................

8. Which base's shape looks like a house?.................

9. If you run around all the bases, how many
   do you touch?...

10. Who wants a frozen fruit pop?............................

Answers: **1.** Baseball **2.** To have fun **3.** Catch the ball **4.** Friends **5.** Pencil, rocket **6.** First **7.** Second **8.** Home plate **9.** Four **10.** Everyone!

Autographs Of Your Favorite Players

Get A Free Baseball Card!

Tell us what your favorite part of baseball practice was, or draw
a picture and mail it to us with a self addressed stamped envelope to:
The Hometown All Stars P.O. Box 235, Woodstock, New York, 12498.

Here are some words we have learned so far.

Bat
Ball
Bases
Catching
Glove
Home Plate
Practice
Lefty
Righty
Throwing
Uniform

Answer to page 7 and 8 is 19 balls, including Billy.